RUH-ROH!
The Mystery of Chemical Reactions!

by Ailynn Collins

CAPSTONE PRESS
a capstone imprint

Published by Capstone Press, an imprint of Capstone
1710 Roe Crest Drive, North Mankato, Minnesota 56003
capstonepub.com

Copyright © 2025 Hanna-Barbera.

SCOOBY-DOO and all related characters and elements are trademarks of and © Hanna-Barbera. (s25)

Library of Congress Cataloging-in-Publication Data is available on the Library of Congress website.

ISBN: 9781669084747 (hardcover)
ISBN: 9781669084693 (paperback)
ISBN: 9781669084709 (ebook PDF)

Summary: Dive into the kitchen with Scooby-Doo and the Mystery Inc. gang for a delicious exploration of chemical reactions. From mixing to melting, see how everyday cooking is full of surprising science! With a sprinkle of classic humor, a dash of fascinating facts, and a dollop of eye-catching illustrations, this Scooby-Doo! Science Adventures whips up the perfect recipe for fun learning.

Editorial Credits
Editor: Donald Lemke; Designer: Tracy Davies; Media Researcher: Svetlana Zhurkin; Production Specialist: Whitney Schaefer

Image Credits
Getty Images: Hulton Archive, 24, 25 (left), Hulton Archive/Keystone/Davies, 23, MelkiNimages, 28 (top); Shutterstock: Africa Studio, 16 (bottle), 28 (bottom), aiyoshi597, 13 (bottom), 21 (bottom), allme, 17, andregric, 26 (bottom), Andrey_Nikitin, 29, AngieYeoh, 16 (vinegar and baking soda), anutr tosirikul, 14 (bottom), Apple_Mac, 16 (measuring cups and spoons), Awais Hashmi, 9, Cartooncux (beaker), cover and throughout, DC Studio, 5, Everett Collection, 15 (bottom), Gavran333, 16 (safety goggles), GoodFocused, 14 (top), HobbitArt (science icons), cover and throughout, James McDowall, 26 (top), julie deshaies, 25 (right), Kashtanowww, cover (atom), konstantinks, 13 (beaker), Kooto, 20, La Gorda, 19, Leonid Ikan, 21 (top), Maria Martyshova (background), cover and throughout, Mariyana M, 7 (top), Natthawon Chaosakun, 11 (top), New Africa, cover (glass beakers), 8, 10, olepeshkina, 4, pisanstock, 16 (funnel), Sansanorth, 12, sumire8, 11 (bottom), Teguh Mujiono, 7 (middle), Tobik, 6, WBMUL, 18, Wirestock Creators, 15 (top), Zaie, cover (molecule), zizou7, 13 (top); Svetlana Zhurkin, 27

Any additional websites and resources referenced in this book are not maintained, authorized, or sponsored by Capstone. All product and company names are trademarks™ or registered® trademarks of their respective holders.

Table of Contents

INTRODUCTION
Mixing It Up **4**

CHAPTER 1
Chemical Reactions **8**

CHAPTER 2
Types of Reactions **12**

CHAPTER 3
Everyday Reactions **18**

CHAPTER 4
Reactions in Action! **22**

Glossary 30
Read More 31
Internet Sites 31
Index 32
About the Author 32

INTRODUCTION

Mixing It Up

Scooby-Doo and Shaggy are in the kitchen, ready to bake a cake. The counter is covered with flour, sugar, eggs, and all kinds of yummy ingredients. Scooby looks at the ingredients, confused. Shaggy tells him that if they mix everything together and bake it—*BAM!*—they'll have a cake.

Scooby thinks it's magic, but Velma explains it's really chemical reactions. Shaggy is surprised to learn they're eating chemicals! Scooby lets out a funny, "Ruh-roh!"

Finally, they mix the ingredients together, amazed at how simple ingredients can make something so tasty.

When we combine ingredients like flour and sugar or pasta and sauce, we get mixtures. Mixtures are made by combining two or more different things. Scientists call this a physical change. You can still separate the items in the mix.

Other examples of physical changes include water turning into ice or mixing sand and pebbles together. The changes here are only in shape, size, or state.

But when substances combine (like when baking a cake), you get something completely different from the original ingredients. These new creations are called **compounds**. Another example of a compound is water, which is made from hydrogen and oxygen **atoms**.

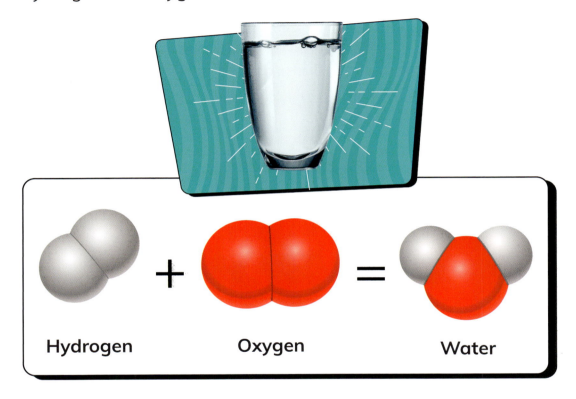

Hydrogen + Oxygen = Water

When substances combine to make a new substance, we call this a chemical change. The change is the result of a chemical reaction.

FACT
The substances used in a chemical reaction are called reactants. The new substances that come out of the reaction are called products.

CHAPTER 1
Chemical Reactions

Everything in the universe is made of matter, and matter is made of tiny particles called atoms and **molecules**. Elements are made of one type of atom. Molecules are groups of atoms stuck together. Got that, gang?

Atoms and molecules have strong **bonds**. For example, two oxygen atoms stick together to form oxygen gas.

Like, who turned out the lights?!

In a chemical reaction, the bonds between atoms break. They join with other atoms to make a new substance. Usually, heat is involved.

Burning is a great example of a chemical reaction. When you light a match, there's smoke, and the stick turns black. The matchstick can't be used again.

FACT

The periodic table is a chart of all the elements scientists know about today. These elements are the building blocks of everything in our world.

How do you know a chemical reaction has happened?

Look for a change in temperature or color. See if a gas has formed or a new substance is left behind. Sometimes, chemical reactions make a strong smell too.

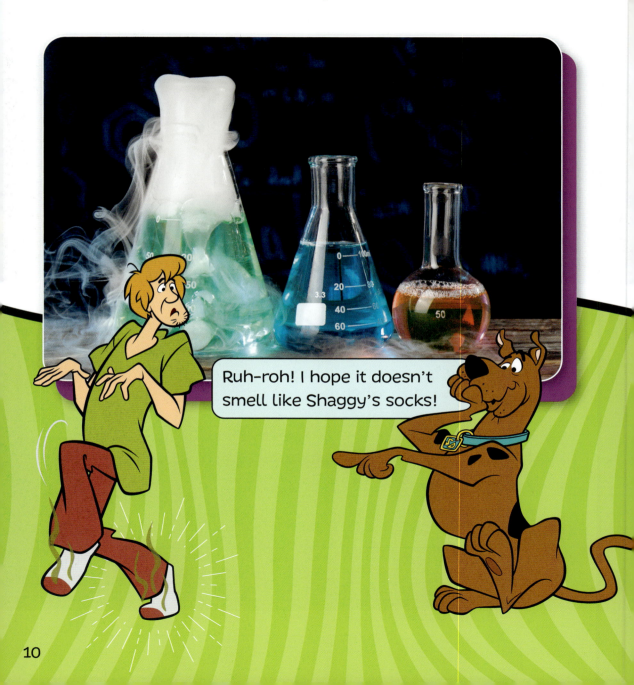

It's an eggs-periment!

Cooking an egg is a great example of a chemical reaction. The egg changes color, and a new substance is formed.

Cooking is all about chemical reactions!

Types of Reactions

There are three main types of chemical reactions: synthesis, **decomposition**, and combustion.

Synthesis means to combine. A synthesis reaction happens when two or more compounds combine to make a new, more complex substance. For example, when hydrogen and oxygen combine, they make water. Another example is when oxygen, iron, and water get together and make rust.

Oxygen + Iron + Water → Rust

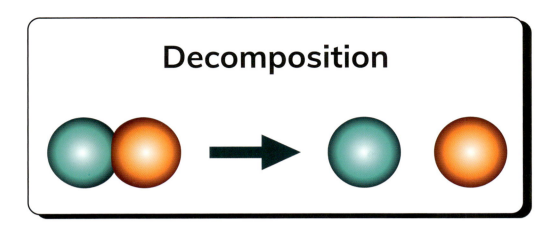

On the other hand, decomposition occurs when a compound breaks down into two or more simpler substances. It's like taking apart a puzzle into smaller pieces!

This usually happens with the help of light, heat, or electricity. For example, when baking soda is heated, it breaks down into water, **carbon dioxide**, and sodium carbonate.

And finally . . . combustion! This reaction happens when a compound reacts with oxygen gas to release energy. The energy is often in the form of heat and light.

Roasting marshmallows is an example of combustion. The marshmallows turn brown but don't catch on fire, releasing hydrogen gas and water vapor in the process.

Other examples of combustion include lighting fireworks or burning gasoline in a car engine to release carbon dioxide and water vapor.

FACT

In 1937, a giant airship called the *Hindenburg* burst into flames. It was filled with hydrogen gas. This gas combined with oxygen in the air, creating a combustion reaction and setting the airship aflame.

Making Baking Soda Fizz

WHAT YOU'LL NEED:

safety goggles
cookie tray
clear plastic bottle
1 tablespoon baking soda
food coloring (optional)
1/4 cup vinegar
funnel
paper towels (for cleanup)

WHAT TO DO:

1. Place the cookie tray on a table to catch spills and keep the area clean.
2. Put the bottle on the tray.
3. Spoon the baking soda into the bottle.
4. Add a couple drops of food coloring to the vinegar if you like.
5. Place the funnel into the opening of the bottle. Then, slowly pour the vinegar into the funnel.
6. Observe what happens next. Does it look like a volcano erupting?

WHAT JUST HAPPENED?

Baking soda is made of sodium, hydrogen, carbon, and oxygen molecules. When it mixes with an acid like vinegar, a fun chemical reaction happens. The combination makes water, carbon dioxide, and carbonic acid. The fizz and bubbling you see is the gas escaping from the mixture!

Rizzy!

CHAPTER 3

Everyday Reactions

Back in the kitchen, the Mystery Inc. gang gathers to eat the cake that Shaggy and Scooby baked. Scooby takes a supersized bite. Chocolate smears across his extra-wide grin. "Rummy!" he barks happily.

Velma, always the scientist, says, "Right now, chemical reactions are turning this food into energy!"

Eating food is the start of many chemical reactions. First, your body digests the food. **Enzymes** in your saliva break down the starches in food into simpler sugars called glucose.

As you swallow, food moves into your stomach and small intestine. More enzymes break down the food even more. In the intestine, tiny finger-like structures absorb those nutrients into your blood.

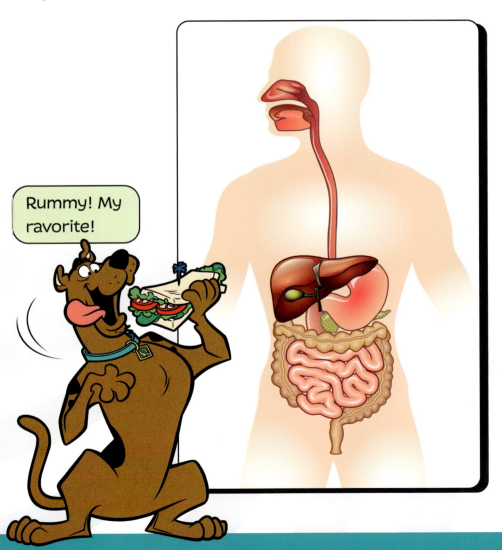

Inside your cells, thousands of chemical reactions happen all the time. Some of these reactions give you energy. Others need that energy to happen. Your body needs energy to keep going—just like the Mystery Machine needs gas!

Sugars in your body break down into carbon dioxide and water, making energy. Every time you eat, the many reactions give you the energy to do what you love.

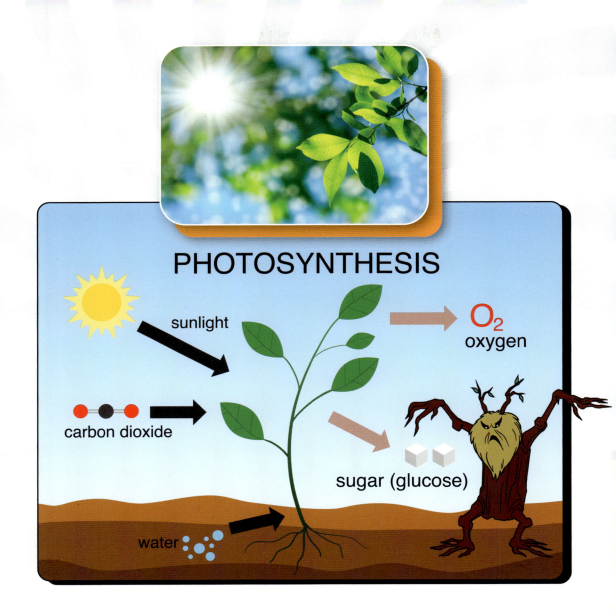

Plants do something similar in a process called **photosynthesis**. It's a well-known example of a synthesis reaction. Plants take in carbon dioxide, water, and sunlight to create food for the plants to grow.

CHAPTER 4

Reactions in Action!

What do batteries, TV screens, and plastic have in common? They're all made possible by chemical reactions. That's right, gang! In fact, chemical reactions are behind many great inventions that make our lives better today.

Alexander Fleming

There have been many famous chemists who did important work for our world. One of them is Alexander Fleming. In 1928, he discovered penicillin. This became a very important medicine. Without it, many people would have died from simple infections.

FACT

Scientists who work with chemical reactions are called chemists.

Marie Curie

Another important chemist was Marie Curie. In the late 1800s, she discovered the elements radium and polonium. Her work with **radioactivity** helped develop X-ray machines. She was the first woman to win a Nobel Prize and is still the only person to have won Nobel Prizes in two sciences.

Dmitri Mendeleev is known for creating the periodic table of the elements. His table organized the elements to show patterns in their properties. Scientists still use this table today to understand how elements behave and relate to each other.

Dmitri Mendeleev

Using Invisible Ink

WHAT YOU'LL NEED:

3 tablespoons lemon juice
small bowl
paintbrush
paper
ironing board
iron

WHAT TO DO:

1. Pour lemon juice into a small bowl.
2. Using the paintbrush, paint a secret message on the paper with the lemon juice. (Don't forget—the message will be invisible!)
3. Let the message dry.
4. Once dry, place the piece of paper on the ironing board.
5. With an adult's help, press the hot iron onto the paper over the message.

Watch what happens. This is a great way to pass secret messages!

WHAT JUST HAPPENED?

Lemon juice is made of carbon compounds that are colorless at room temperature. When heated with an iron, the compounds release carbon. Carbon mixes with oxygen in the air and turns darker, revealing the secret message.

Keep exploring the wonderful world of chemical reactions by observing things that happen in everyday life. From baking a cake to the way plants grow, chemical reactions are happening all around. These reactions help us understand the world better and can even lead to amazing discoveries.

So keep asking questions, gang! Stay curious, and never stop exploring the amazing world of science. Who knows? Maybe one day you'll make a groundbreaking discovery of your own!

GLOSSARY

atom (AT-uhm)—the smallest particle of an element

bond (BAHND)—to hold together

carbon dioxide (KAR-bon die-OK-side)—a gas that people and animals breathe out and plants use to make food

compound (KOM-pound)—substance made when two or more elements are joined together, like water

decomposition (dee-kom-puh-ZISH-un)—when something breaks down into simpler parts, like a leaf rotting into soil

enzyme (EN-zime)—a special protein that helps speed up chemical reactions in the body

molecule (MOL-uh-kyool)—group of atoms bonded together, making up the smallest part of a compound

photosynthesis (foh-toh-SIN-thuh-sis)—the process plants use to turn sunlight, water, and air into food

radioactivity (ray-dee-oh-ak-TIV-uh-tee)—the energy released when the center of an atom breaks apart

READ MORE

Biskup, Agnieszka. *The Dynamic World of Chemical Reactions with Max Axiom, Super Scientist.* North Mankato, MN: Capstone, 2019.

Peterson, Megan Cooley. *Scooby-Doo! A Science of Chemical Reactions Mystery: The Overreacting Ghost.* North Mankato, MN: Capstone, 2017.

Weakland, Mark. *Kaboom!: Wile E. Coyote Experiments with Chemical Reactions.* North Mankato, MN: Capstone, 2017.

INTERNET SITES

Britannica Kids: Chemical Reaction
kids.britannica.com/students/article/chemical-reaction/623708

Ducksters: Solids, Liquids, and Gases
ducksters.com/science/solids_liquids_gases.php

STEMful: Spark, Pop, Fizz! Chemical Reaction Experiments for Younger Kids
sf-stemful.com/what-is-a-chemical-reaction

INDEX

atoms, 7, 8, 9

carbon dioxide, 13, 15, 17, 20, 21

chemists, 23–24
combustion, 12, 14, 15
compounds, 7, 12, 27
Curie, Marie, 24

decomposition, 12, 13

energy, 14, 18, 20
enzymes, 19

Fleming, Alexander, 23

hydrogen, 7, 12, 14, 15, 17

Mendeleev, Dmitri, 25
mixtures, 6
molecules, 8, 17

oxygen, 7, 8, 12, 14, 15, 17, 27

periodic table, 9, 25
photosynthesis, 21

substances, 7, 13
synthesis, 12, 21

water, 6, 7, 12, 13, 14, 15, 17, 20, 21

ABOUT THE AUTHOR

Ailynn Collins has written many books for children, from stories about aliens and monsters, to books about science, space, and the future. These are her favorite subjects. She lives outside Seattle with her family and 5 dogs. When she's not writing, she enjoys participating in dog shows and dog sports.